Franklin's Rocket Team

Kids Can Press

FRANKLIN loved camping. He loved everything to do with outer space, too. So he was super excited to invite Rabbit to camp out in his new rocket ship tent.

"These will help you steer," said Mr. Turtle, attaching a set of fins to the side of the rocket.

"And this will make a perfect satellite dish," said Franklin as he tried to balance a foil plate on top of one of the fins.

The satellite dish wobbled and then fell to the ground.

"If I can get it to stay up," Franklin added.

"There!" said Franklin when he finally managed to balance the satellite dish. "Now I'm all set for Rabbit."

Just then, Harriet raced into the yard. "Look at me!" she said. "I can run fast, just like Rabbit."

"Watch out!" Franklin and Mr. Turtle shouted. But they were too late. Harriet bumped the satellite dish, and it toppled over.

"Oops!" she said. "Sorry, Franklin."

"Sisters," sighed Franklin.

"Don't worry, Franklin," said Mr. Turtle. "I'll help you fix it."

Later that afternoon, Mr. Turtle greeted Rabbit at the door.
"Hi, Mr. Turtle," Rabbit said shyly. "Thanks for having me over."

"Rabbit!" Harriet said as she raced up to him. "Yay!"

Rabbit smiled. "Hi, Harri-Harri-Harriet!"

"Hi, Rab-Rab-Rabbit!" Harriet giggled.

"Come on in, Rabbit," said Franklin. "Let's put your things away so we can go play rocket ship!"

"Safe space travels, kids!" Mr. Turtle said.

Franklin took Rabbit to his room. Harriet followed closely behind.

"Hi, Goldie," Rabbit said, peering into her fishbowl. "How-*glub*-are-*glub*-you-*glub*?"

Then Rabbit put his ear to the bowl as if he were listening to Goldie. "She says she's '*Glub, glub, glub* … wet!'"

Harriet giggled. "Again!" she said.

"Not now, Harriet," said Franklin. "I need to show Rabbit all of our space stuff."

Rabbit smiled at Harriet and followed Franklin out into the backyard.

"That's our rocket ship," said Franklin, pointing at the tent. "And that's our satellite dish." He pointed at the foil plate.

"Coolio!" said Rabbit.

"This is a laser for when it gets dark," said Franklin, holding up a flashlight. "And these are zero-gravity grabbers!" He handed Rabbit a pair of pot lids.

"This is going to be the best sleepover ever!" said Rabbit.

"Rabbit!" called Harriet. "I brought you a snack."

"Thanks," said Rabbit. He took a radish and balanced it on his nose.

Harriet giggled.

"It's time for you to go inside, Harriet," Franklin said.

"But I want to play with Rabbit," Harriet said.

"Come on, Harriet," said Rabbit, holding out his hand. "I'll walk you in."

"Okay!" said Harriet. As she bounced over to him, she knocked the tent, and the satellite dish fell over. Again.

"Harriet!" shouted Franklin. "Why can't you be careful?"

"It's okay, Franklin," said Rabbit. "I'll help you fix it in a minute."

"*Hmph,*" Franklin said.

Franklin spent a long time trying to fix the satellite dish. By the time he got it balanced again, the sun was setting, and Rabbit still hadn't come back. So Franklin went inside to look for him.

Franklin found Rabbit having a tea party with Harriet. "Rabbit, can we go play rocket ship now?" he asked.

"Sure," said Rabbit. "Just let me finish my tea."

Franklin sighed and waited.

With one last sip Rabbit said, "Spaceman Rabbit, ready for duty!"

Franklin and Rabbit raced back to the rocket ship.

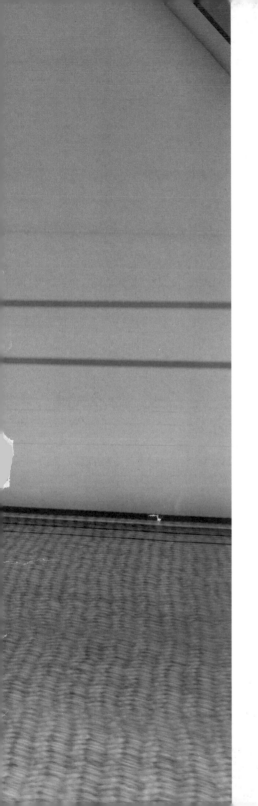

In the tent, Franklin and Rabbit prepared for takeoff.

"10, 9, 8 ..." Franklin counted down.

But the countdown was interrupted.

"Hi, Rabbit!" said Harriet, popping her head into the rocket ship.

"Not now, Harriet!" said Franklin.

"But we want to go to space, too," said Harriet. She lined up her toys against the tent wall.

"Hey!" Rabbit said, his eyes lighting up. "The toys can be our space crew! And Harriet can be our first officer!"

"No!" shouted Franklin, storming off. "This is not how you play rocket ship!"

Franklin stomped into the kitchen. "Harriet is such a pest!" he said.

"What's wrong?" asked Mr. Turtle.

"I can't play rocket ship with Rabbit because Harriet keeps butting in," said Franklin.

"Harriet just wants to be part of the fun," said Mrs. Turtle.

"Well, it isn't fun for me!" said Franklin.

"It *is* almost her bedtime," Mr. Turtle said. "How about I keep her busy until then?"

"Thanks, Dad," said Franklin.

Franklin and Mr. Turtle headed back to the tent together.

When Franklin and Mr. Turtle got to the tent, Rabbit and Harriet were playing with Harriet's toys.

"That sure looks like fun," said Mr. Turtle. "But I really wish I could go to a tea party …"

"A tea party?" said Harriet. "I'll have a tea party with you, Daddy!"
"Great," Mr. Turtle said, winking at Franklin.
"Come on, Daddy!" said Harriet. "Let's go!"
Franklin gave his dad the thumbs-up.

"Sorry for storming off," Franklin said to Rabbit. "Harriet was being a real pain."

"I understand," said Rabbit. "Sometimes my little brothers and sisters bug me, too." He reached into his overnight bag and pulled out a family photo.

"Wow, you have a huge family!" said Franklin.

"Yep," said Rabbit. "It's kind of strange being here without them all. I miss them."

"So that's why you want to play with Harriet," said Franklin, smiling. "In that case, I think I know just how to make you feel better …"

"A space tea party was a great idea, Franklin!" said Rabbit.

"Yeah!" said Harriet. She did a twirl and knocked over the satellite dish. Again. "Oops! Sorry, Franklin."

"That's okay," said Franklin, putting the foil plate on his head. "It makes a better tea party hat, anyway!"